THE SNOW BEAR

D0674992

tiger tales

5 River Road, Suite 128, Wilton, CT 06897
Published in the United States 2019
Originally published in Great Britain 2012
as *The Snow Bear* by the Little Tiger Group
Text copyright © 2012 Holly Webb
Illustrations copyright © 2012 Artful Doodlers
Cover illustrations copyright © 2012 Simon Mendez
Photographic images courtesy of www.shutterstock.com
ISBN-13: 978-1-68010-446-2
ISBN-10: 1-68010-446-2
Printed in China
STP/1800/0259/0319
10 9 8 7 6 5 4 3 2 1

For more insight and activities, visit us at www.tigertalesbooks.com

THE
SNOW
BEAR

by HOLLY WEBB

tiger tales

For Tom, Robin, and William,
and for Phoebe, who loves polar bears.

~ HOLLY WEBB

Contents

CHAPTER ONE

Christmas at Grandpa's

"Look, Grandpa! It's starting to snow!" Sara peered out the window, watching the first flakes spiral lazily down.

Grandpa looked up from the pile of old black-and-white photos he was sorting through and nodded. "So it is. Well, they did say on the news that it might."

Sara frowned. "Do you think it'll be snowing at home?"

"Could be. It's likely to be worse here, though. We're farther north. And the winds from the ocean make it a lot colder, too." He got up and came to sit on the wide windowsill next to Sara. "Why are you looking worried? You love it when it snows!"

Sara nodded. It was true that some of her best memories of winter trips to Grandpa's house were of playing in the snow. But then Mom and Dad had been there, too. She couldn't have a snowball fight on her own.

"I hope it isn't snowing back home," she muttered, leaning against Grandpa's shoulder. "What if the baby comes and Mom and Dad can't get to the hospital?"

"The baby isn't due until after Christmas," he said comfortingly. "And anyway, they'd call an ambulance. Ambulance crews manage, you know. They're trained in that sort of thing."

"I suppose." Sara gave herself a little shake. There was no point worrying. She'd just remind Dad to put a shovel in the trunk when he called later, that was all.

"It's piling up!" she told Grandpa as she watched the flakes falling faster and faster. They were staying on the windowsill outside now, not just melting away as soon as they touched it. She wriggled closer to the glass and peered up as the snowflakes whirled past. The light was fading, and the sky was a strange grayish-yellow color, as though there was a lot more snow up there.

"Mm-hm. Looks like it," Grandpa agreed. "I think I've done enough work for this afternoon. Should we go and find something to make for dinner?" He kissed the top of her head, laughing. "It's all right. There *are* windows in the kitchen, too. You'll still be able to see the snow. If it really piles up, you'll be able to go out and play in it tomorrow. It's too late now, though; it's getting dark already."

Sara slid down from the windowsill with a tiny sigh. She loved Grandpa and his strange old house. It was made of stone, built more than 200 years ago, and it had a huge fireplace and deep windows that were perfect for sitting in. All the floors sloped and wobbled, and it was full of strange little hiding places. But if she was at home, she'd get to go out in the snow with all her friends who lived close by. They'd build snowmen in the park and have snowball fights, and then go back to each other's houses to warm up. But she didn't really want to build a snowman by herself, and it wouldn't be quite the same just with Grandpa.

Sara and her mom and dad always came to Grandpa's house at the beginning of Christmas vacation. It was a tradition. They'd stay for a few days, and then they'd all go back home for Christmas, Grandpa, too. But this year, Mom and Dad had decided it was better if Sara went to stay with Grandpa on her own. Dad had driven her up, stayed for a quick lunch, and headed home again.

Mom wasn't able to travel far at all— she was due to have Sara's baby brother a brother a couple of weeks after Christmas, and she didn't want to be squashed in a car for hours. Plus it wasn't very smart for her to be in an old stone house on a clifftop by the ocean, down a long bumpy track, miles and miles from town, let alone a hospital. Sara loved the feeling she got at Grandpa's of being far away from anywhere. His house was like a safe little nest up on the cliff, like the seabirds' nests he'd shown her when they stayed in the summer. But she had to admit it wasn't the right place for Mom right now.

"Does it snow like this in the far north in Canada?" Sara asked Grandpa as she followed him out of his study and down the murky half-light of the hallway to the kitchen. Grandpa had turned the lights on, but it was still gloomy. "In the Arctic, where you and Great-Grandpa were? Does it look like the same kind of snow?"

Grandpa turned around from the fridge. "Snow's snow, mostly, Sara. We saw some real blizzards there, though. There was one that lasted for three days once, and we were caught by it while we were visiting one of the Inuit families. My dad and I had supplies back at our own house that we'd brought with us—tins of stew, that kind of thing—but these people were living on their traditional foods." Grandpa paused, looking at Sara hopefully, waiting for her to ask. Sara didn't mind. She loved his stories.

"What did you have to eat?"

"Dried seal meat," Grandpa told her triumphantly, pulling a bag of spaghetti out of the cupboard. He waved a jar of pasta sauce at her. "Nothing like this. No pasta one day, stir-fry the next. With maybe a nice roast chicken on a Sunday. The Inuit mostly eat seal meat through the winter, and usually they have it raw. Maybe some fish. Caribou meat in the summer. Whale meat and blubber, too, of course."

Sara shuddered. Blubber was fat, and she hated the idea of having to eat it. She cut all the fat off her meat, and Grandpa teased her about it. He said she'd be useless in a cold climate. "You *really* ate blubber?"

"We had to," Grandpa nodded. "That blizzard lasted days. There wasn't anything else, and we were hungry. Besides, it would have been rude to say no. They were sharing their food with us. How could we say we didn't want it when it was so precious to them?"

It seemed colder in the kitchen suddenly, and Sara shivered. The snow was building up around the corners of the window over the sink. She didn't want to think about being shut in with a blizzard screaming outside, even in this cozy house. "Were you in an igloo?" she asked.

"Yes, a big one, made to last for the whole winter. It still wasn't any taller than your great-grandpa, though. Almost all of it was the sleeping area. And there were six of us in there."

"For three days…," Sara muttered. It couldn't have been bigger than her bedroom at home. "You must have been really annoyed with each other, being shut in all together."

Grandpa smiled. "It helped me with learning the language, though. They told so many stories over those few days."

"Stories like the ones you're writing down?" Sara asked. Grandpa was writing a book on Inuit folktales. He'd been fascinated by them ever since he'd lived in Canada, when he was only a few years older than Sara. His father, Sara's great-grandfather, had gone there to study the Inuit people and taken his son with him. The house was full of the amazing things Great-Grandpa had brought back, and Grandpa, too, when he'd returned to the Canadian Arctic years later.

Grandpa nodded. "It was those three days of stories that got me started. When the blizzard finally died down and we came out of the igloo, it was as if they were all swirling around in my head. Some of them I didn't understand—there are many Inuit languages, and even your great-grandpa didn't know all the different ones. I don't know them all now. I just got pieces of those stories here and there. Little snippets. Men who turned into polar bears. Strange gods and goddesses.

Amazing things…."

Sara smiled at him. "Tell me the polar bear story. The one about you and your friend, while you're making dinner. Please?"

"That one again?" Grandpa laughed. "You're just like your dad. It was always his favorite, too."

Sara nodded. She loved imagining Grandpa telling the story to Dad, too. It was a family story—it belonged to her, and Dad, and Grandpa. It had been Great-Grandpa's, too. It was special. "I wish I could go there and see it all…," she said wistfully. "The igloos, and the seals, and the polar bears."

Grandpa shook his head. "I don't think you'd see an igloo now, Sara. Most Inuit people live in houses these days. Even back when Great-Grandpa and I were there, igloos were rare. That's why we went. We wanted to record it all, before it changed forever."

"Forever?" Sara asked sadly.

"I think so," Grandpa agreed with a sigh. "Things do change. But sometimes for the better."

CHAPTER
TWO

A Polar Tale

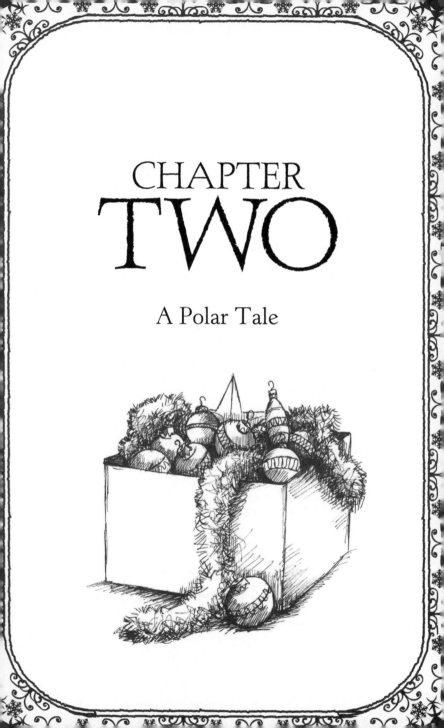

"So … the polar bear." Grandpa smiled at Sara. "Are you sure? You know the story is a little sad."

"Yes! I love it. I love that it's about you."

Grandpa nodded. "Actually, the family that we were with during the blizzard was my friend Alignak and his older brother, his father, and his grandmother. The same Alignak who was with me when we found the polar bear cub."

"How old was he?" Sara asked, sitting down at the kitchen table. "The bear, I mean."

"Alignak thought he was just a couple of months old. We found him in the springtime—he said that the cub couldn't have been out of his den for long. He'd seen cubs before. I hadn't a clue. The bear was just sitting in the snow, looking miserable."

"What were you doing when you found him?"

Grandpa laughed. "Well, Alignak was out to catch fish. I was along for the trip. He thought I was really funny. Useless at everything useful."

"And you found a polar bear." Sara giggled. "What did Alignak's mom say when he came home with a bear instead of fish?"

Grandpa shook his head. "His mom had died, years before. It was a hard place to live, Sara. Alignak's grandmother took care of him, and his dad and his brother."

Sara nodded. "I remember now. Was his grandmother surprised?"

"Alignak had brought creatures home before—an Arctic hare once. But never a bear. She told us to take it back. And Alignak told her he couldn't, because he'd used up all the dried fish she'd given him, coaxing the bear cub to follow us home. She was furious with him about that. But the bear stayed. Alignak and I had to fish to feed him, and his father and brother gave us seal meat and blubber sometimes, too. I think he was probably too young for most of the things he ate. His mother would still have been giving him her milk. But he was hungry, so he made do."

"What did you call him?" Sara asked. She knew already, but she liked Grandpa to tell her—it was part of the story.

"Peter. I named him, and Alignak liked the sound of it."

It was an old-fashioned name, but Sara liked it, too.

"What happened?" she asked quietly. This was the sad part.

Grandpa sighed. "We kept him all through the spring and the summer, and he got bigger. Alignak's father wasn't happy about the amount of food he was eating. He was taking food away from the family. And looking back, I think they were worried that Peter might hurt us. Never on purpose—he was friendlier than a dog. But even though he was only the size of a small dog when we found him, he was getting bigger and bigger, and he was strong. He'd jump up to hug us, and we'd go flying. He didn't really understand that his teeth and claws were too sharp for playing." Grandpa chuckled. "Actually, they weren't too sharp—it was just that we weren't bears. He should have been wrestling with his brother or sister. Polar bears usually have twins, and they grow up playing together."

Sara nodded. "So you had to make him go away."

"We first tried to teach him how to catch seals. We didn't want him to be on his own without being able to hunt. We showed him good places to find birds' eggs." Grandpa leaned closer, showing her a tiny red mark at the side of his cheek. "See this scar? That's from an Arctic tern. They were dive-bombing us—you couldn't blame them, really. We were stealing their eggs. Peter loved them."

He sighed again. "It still makes me sad. We waited until the winter was coming— once the ocean was frozen over, it would be easier for Peter to catch seals from the ice. He was almost a year old then, we guessed, when we left him there. Just about old enough to take care of himself. Probably."

"But he would have died if you hadn't taken him home with you when you found him," Sara said firmly. "You did the right thing."

Grandpa nodded. "I know. And it wasn't fair to ask Alignak's family to take care of a bear."

"Did you ever see him again?"

Grandpa stirred the pasta thoughtfully. "We thought we did. There were quite a few young bears around that winter. But we could never be sure. I worried that he'd have gone too close to another polar bear without realizing. Polar bears are loners once they're grown-up. Not friendly to each other. And after that winter, our year was up. We came home here again, your great-grandpa and me." He glanced at Sara. "Come and watch this pasta for a moment. I've got something I think you'd like to see. I found it earlier, mixed in with some other old things." He went out to the study again and came back a few minutes later with an old black-and-white photo. "Look."

Sara took it carefully. "Grandpa! Is that you?"

"Mm-hm. And Alignak, and Peter. Sixty years ago, that must be now."

The boys and the bear stared out of the picture at Sara, smiling. Even the bear was smiling, she was sure.

Sara sat by Grandpa's fireplace after dinner, toasting in the warmth of the flames and gazing at the photograph, where Grandpa had propped it up on the mantel. The two boys looked so happy.

But seeing them just made her feel

lonely. Grandpa was doing his best, but she missed Mom and Dad. It felt so strange being at Grandpa's house without them.

Grandpa was out in the shed, finding the special holder they were going to put the Christmas tree in. It was Sara's job to decorate it. But she needed Dad to help her get the garland right up to the top. And Mom always pointed out the branches that still needed ornaments. It just wasn't the same. Sara sniffed.

Iknik, Grandpa's beautiful orange cat, stalked into the room. He came over and sat down in front of the fire, close to Sara, but she was pretty sure it was the heat he wanted, not her. He wasn't really a friendly cat, although for some reason he would always sit on Sara's mom. Grandpa said it was because Iknik was ornery, and he could tell that Sara's mom didn't like cats very much. Sara thought he was probably right. Still, *she* loved cats, and she kept trying with Iknik.

"Hey, Iknik…," she muttered. "Here, kitty, kitty."

Iknik turned his head and glared at her with eyes that glinted reddish-gold in the firelight. They made him look fierce, and Sara dropped her hand. She'd been about to pet him, but maybe it wasn't a good idea.

"Found it!" Grandpa called. He looked triumphant as he dragged in the tree holder. "You're in early, Iknik. He's usually out hunting this time of the evening, but maybe he doesn't like the snow. He's probably forgotten it since last year. Unless it's because I've lit the fire." He came over to rub Iknik behind the ears. "I originally called him Iknik because it means fire, and he had such fiery marmalade fur, and those strange

34

yellowish eyes. But it's an even better name than I meant it to be. Sometimes I worry he's going to singe his whiskers, but he seems to know just how close he can get."

Iknik purred and rubbed the side of his head against Grandpa's pants. Sara sighed. He wouldn't ever do that to her.

She stared gloomily into the fire. She wanted to be cheerful—she really didn't want to upset Grandpa and make him think she wasn't having a good time. Especially as Grandpa might worry and think he should call Dad. Which would make him and Mom worry about her, too.

But it was so hard to be happy when she just wasn't.

Grandpa put his arm around her shoulders. "Do you think it's time for bed? You might even wake up to find everything covered in snow…."

CHAPTER
THREE

Sara's Snow Bear

Sara woke up the next morning feeling cold. Grandpa's house was wonderful, but the radiators were ancient, and sometimes they didn't work as well as they should. The room felt cold, and somehow *looked* cold, too, she realized, as she hauled her comforter up around her shoulders. The bedroom she slept in at Grandpa's was her dad's old one, but Grandpa had repainted it. When her dad had it, it was covered in posters, Grandpa said, and you could hardly see the blue paint. He'd decorated it a pale pink when Sara was little. But today the pink walls didn't seem as warm and rosy as usual. There was an icy, crystal feeling in the air.

"The snow!" Sara squeaked, jumping out of bed, and then squeaking again at the coldness of the wooden floorboards. "Ow, ow…." She hopped across the floor on her toes, dragging the comforter with her, and climbed up onto the windowsill. It was a large one, almost like a window seat, and she liked to curl up in it and read. She flung the curtains open and took a deep, delighted breath. "Oh, look at it…."

Grandpa's yard was very big, but usually Sara knew where everything was—the clumps of rosebushes, the wooden bench, the birdbath. Now it was all just lumps and bumps. Even the birdbath seemed to have disappeared in the deep, sparkling snow.

She glanced around as the hall floorboards creaked. Grandpa beamed at her from the bedroom door. "I might have known you'd be awake already. Amazing, isn't it?"

"It's so thick," Sara agreed. "I don't think I've ever seen snow like this."

"It must have snowed heavily all night," Grandpa said, coming to stand at the window with her. "And the wind's been blowing the snow around, too. It's all banked up against the wall."

Sara nodded. That explained why everything looked so strange. She hadn't thought about the wind; she'd just expected that snow fell straight down. But of course it didn't. It flurried around. "The wall looks like a ski jump," she said, giggling. "Can I go out in it, Grandpa? I have my big coat and boots."

Grandpa nodded. "Are you sure you don't want breakfast first? It might warm you up."

Sara shook her head. There was

something about the perfect glittering whiteness outside—she wanted to go and run around in it and see her footprints. "I'll come back for breakfast in a little while. Is that okay? I just want to see what it's like."

Grandpa nodded. "I think I'll make scrambled eggs. You'll need something hot. I feel cold just looking at all that snow."

"But it can't be as cold as it was in the Arctic," Sara reminded him.

"Mm-hm. I'm 60 years older than I was then, Sara. The cold seems to seep into my bones now. Still, maybe later on, when I've had some breakfast, I'll come out in it with you."

Sara hurried to get dressed, putting on her warmest sweater and pants, and a pair of thick socks to go under her boots. If she hadn't promised her mom that she really would brush her teeth every morning, she would have skipped that, but she felt too guilty.

Teeth brushed, she rushed down the stairs and opened the back door. The wind had slowed down, and the air was very still. It made walking out into the yard seem dreamlike because it was so quiet. The snow had hushed everything. Even the ocean, which Sara could always hear beating against the rocks when she stayed with Grandpa. It was just a soft whisper in the background.

The yard looked like an illustration from a fairy tale. Sara had seen snow before, of course, but this was so deep, and so clean and new, that everything shimmered and sparkled in the thin, clear sunlight.

"I hope it doesn't melt," Sara said to herself, glancing up at the sky. But it didn't feel like it would. The sunshine hardly had any warmth in it, and she was cold, even wrapped up in her coat and long scarf. She stepped out onto the grass. At least, she thought it was the grass. She had to step carefully—she could have been standing on anything. Sara held out her hands to steady herself. She was glad that Grandpa didn't have a pond—she might walk out into the middle of it in this.

"This is definitely the patch of grass between the roses and the wall," Sara muttered to herself, frowning and trying to remember the layout of the yard. She knew exactly what it looked like, almost as well as she knew her yard at home!

But she'd never tried to walk around it blindfolded, and that was what it felt like.

The snow crunched and squeaked under her boots as she tracked across the lawn, admiring her footprints. It was about eight inches deep, she thought. Not quite high enough to go over the top of her boots. But almost.

Sara turned and looked back at her trail. The prints were really crisp, as though she'd shaped them with a knife. The snow was calling for her to build something in it. But not just a snowman. Somehow that wasn't right for the magical feel of the morning. Sara molded a snowball thoughtfully, pressing it together between her gloved hands, and enjoying the feel of the snow under her fingers.

Then she smiled. Of course. Grandpa's story from last night. She was going to make a snow bear.

Once she had the idea, it came easily. The snow was a little powdery, but it held together well enough, and the shape she had in mind wasn't very complicated. Sara loved polar bears, and she had a bunch of toy ones at home of all sizes, and a little notebook with a polar bear photo on the cover. The bear was sitting up, almost like a boy slouching against a wall, with his hind paws stuck out in front of him. So it was easy enough to heap up a mound of snow to be his back, stretching it out into two big back paws. The head was harder—when she tried to build the snow into a pointed bear face, it just fell off. In the end she rolled a triangular snowball and balanced it on the top, with little snowballs for ears. Then she shaped some of the body into front paws hanging down at the sides.

Sara stood back, admiring her bear. He was almost finished, but there was something missing. She pursed her lips thoughtfully, and then sighed. The eyes. She needed some little stones, or something like that—but everything was buried under the snow. She glanced around and managed to find a couple of dark, withered rose leaves, still just about visible under the snow covering the bushes. She pushed them into place on either side of the long white muzzle, but they didn't look quite right.

Someone laughed behind her, and she turned to see Grandpa standing in the doorway.

"He's fantastic, Sara!"

She grinned at him. "He is nice," she agreed. "But he isn't finished, Grandpa. His face looks wrong. It's mostly the eyes. I can't find anything to make them out of."

Grandpa nodded, and then rubbed his hands together. "I know. Give me just a minute." He hurried indoors and came back smiling, holding out a hand to her.

Sara tramped to the door, feeling the cold now that she'd stopped building. "Oh, they're perfect," she said delightedly, picking the pieces of green sea glass from Grandpa's hand. "I should have thought of that. Can I really borrow them? Won't they get lost in the snow?"

Grandpa had a jar of sea glass on the kitchen windowsill, all shades of green, and even a couple of tiny blue pieces. He picked it up when he went walking on the beach, and now, when the sun shone through it on the windowsill, it looked like a tiny jarful of the ocean inside the house.

"Of course you can. You'll just have to go hunting on the beach for some more if they disappear when your bear melts. I'm sure we'll see them in the grass, though."

Sara ran back to the bear, taking out the leaves and pressing the green glass into the snow. She smiled at the difference they made to the long white face. He was suddenly real, a snow bear sitting in the yard.

She couldn't help glancing back at him as she hurried in to eat breakfast. She had the strangest feeling that he was waiting for her to return.

CHAPTER
FOUR

Building an Igloo

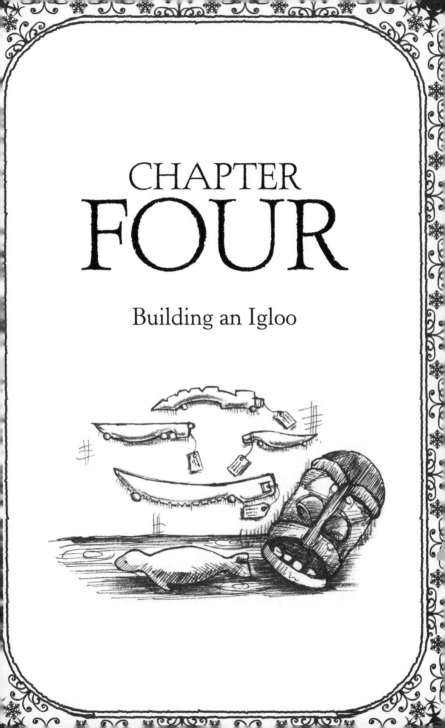

"So what are you going to do now?" Grandpa asked as they finished breakfast, both using the rest of their toast to scoop up the last of the scrambled eggs. "I might be up to a snowball fight, if you're brave enough…."

Sara giggled. "Maybe."

"Or you could make a whole family of bears."

Sara shook her head. "No. One's enough." She looked hopefully at Grandpa. "I'd really like to build an igloo…." She'd been thinking about it while she was eating breakfast—that she needed an igloo to live in next to the bear. It was all part of the story.

Grandpa blinked. "I've never built one, Sara," he admitted. "I've watched it done, but it's very complicated. You have to stamp the snow down and then leave it to freeze before you cut the blocks out and build with them."

"Oh." Sara nodded sadly.

"But actually...." Grandpa got up to look out the kitchen window. "That snow that's been blown against the wall might be hard enough. Because the wind squashed it all against the bricks."

"Really?" Sara asked hopefully, coming to stand on tiptoe beside him, peering out to look.

"Mm-hm. It wouldn't be a very long-lasting one," Grandpa warned. "More of a quick shelter, the kind that Inuit hunters would build if they were away overnight."

"Any kind of igloo—I don't mind," Sara told him.

Grandpa nodded and put their plates in

the sink. "I might even have something that would help," he told her, and Sara followed him into his study. Grandpa stood by the desk, looking at the collection of strange objects mounted on the wall behind it. Sara loved to look at them and try to figure out what the faded old labels said—her great-grandpa had very spidery writing.

"There it is!" Grandpa said triumphantly, taking down a long, toothed knife, not metal, but made of something strange, hard and yellowish.

"What is it?" Sara asked.

"It's a snow knife," Grandpa explained. "See if you can guess what it's made out of."

Sara rubbed her hand along the smooth surface of the knife. It reminded her of teeth, and she frowned worriedly. "It isn't made out of elephant tusks, is it, Grandpa? We were learning about ivory at school, and how people kill elephants just for their tusks."

"Not quite. It isn't from an elephant, but it is a kind of ivory. Do you remember me telling you about walruses? They're like seals, with big tusks."

"And that's what this is made from?" Sara said. She didn't like the idea of a knife made out of teeth.

"A long time ago. Your great-grandpa brought this home, and it would have been very old even then. Walruses are protected now, but back then, hunters and their families used their bones and tusks after they'd eaten the walrus meat. They didn't waste anything. And this knife was for cutting out the blocks of snow to make an igloo."

Sara nodded. It looked a little like the kind of plastic knife she used to cut play dough with. She could see how it would work on snow. "I wonder how many igloos it's made," she said thoughtfully.

"Maybe hundreds. Let's make one more with it, shall we?" Grandpa suggested, going out into the hall and slipping it into the pocket of his thick, padded coat. "I should think your great-grandpa would be delighted. And whoever it was who made the knife."

They went out into the yard, and Sara patted the head of her snow bear, still sitting solemnly in the middle of the snowy lawn.

Grandpa examined the bank of snow by the wall and nodded. "Good and solid, like I thought. Now we have to try and cut it into blocks with the knife."

Sara watched Grandpa with the walrus-ivory knife—she still wasn't quite sure about it. She stomped around the snow they were going to build on, flattening it down, while Grandpa started to cut out thick blocks of solid snow. It looked tricky to do, and Sara was glad they weren't trying to build a big igloo.

When they had the first few blocks, they laid them in a semicircle behind the snow bear so that he would be sitting in front of the igloo.

"And now we just keep stacking them up…," Sara said, looking doubtfully at their ring of blocks.

"Yes, and they'll press in on each other as we curve them—that's the plan, anyway," Grandpa agreed. He was looking excited about the project now, Sara realized.

Sara nodded. She had a feeling the igloo was going to be a lot of hard work. But it would be so amazing if they could really make one big enough to sit in.

After the first ring of blocks, they edged

them in a tiny bit so that the igloo would be dome-shaped, and then the next row a little more. By the third row, the wall was up to Sara's waist, and it was starting to feel like a real little house.

"Wouldn't it be really dark inside if we were making one with just a tiny tunnel to get in?" Sara asked Grandpa, panting a little as she helped him heave a block up to the height of her shoulders.

"Mm-hm," Grandpa agreed. "They'd have an oil lamp, usually—burning oil made from seal fat. That made the igloo work better, too, oddly enough. The heat from the lamp melted the snow on the inside just a little, and then it froze again harder, and that thin layer of ice stuck all the blocks together." He grinned at Sara. "We could try shining a flashlight on the inside of ours, but I'm not sure it would work. The Inuit would have used a seal's tummy to make a window. Stomachs are see-through when you stretch them out! But I don't have one of those, sorry."

"Ughhh!" Sara gave him a disgusted look.

"We might be able to get some ice off the top of the wall, if we feel like being clever. Some igloo-builders would do that," Grandpa explained.

Sara nodded excitedly. "I know we don't really need one, but it would make it even better." She swallowed, trying not to sound upset. "We should take some pictures of it and e-mail them to Mom and Dad."

Grandpa put his arm around her. "Good idea. Your dad would have loved this—we tried building an igloo together once, but the snow was a little too soft." He chuckled to himself. "It collapsed all over me, and your dad couldn't stop laughing. We just had a snowball fight after that."

He sighed. "You're really missing them, aren't you?"

"I'm sorry," Sara whispered. "It just feels funny here without them."

Grandpa nodded. "I know. Sara, love, this snow…." He stopped, looking at her worriedly, and Sara stared back at him.

"What?"

"I'm not sure I'm going to be able to take you home tomorrow."

Sara gasped. She hadn't even thought about that. But of course the roads would all be blocked by snow—the track up to Grandpa's house was so narrow, and even the main road wasn't very wide.

"What about Christmas?" she whispered. "It's only two more days…."

"Well, maybe it'll thaw," Grandpa said, hugging her tighter. "Hopefully.

But I can't promise that it will, Sara, even though I wish I could."

Sara nodded, rubbing her hands over her eyes. It was horrible, crying when it was so cold. The hot tears burned her eyes, and then felt like they were freezing onto her cheeks. "Can I go back inside?" she gulped, not looking up at him. The igloo wasn't done yet, but she couldn't finish it now.

"Of course you can! I'll come and make you some hot chocolate." Grandpa sounded so upset, and that only made Sara feel worse. She bolted into the house, took off her coat, hat, scarf, and boots as fast as she could with frozen fingers, and ran upstairs. She was really cold, but she didn't want a drink. She looked around her room uncertainly, and then dived back into bed, hiding herself under the comforter.

She heard Grandpa opening her bedroom door a few minutes later, but he didn't say anything, and then the floorboards creaked as he slowly went out again.

CHAPTER FIVE

A Story in the Snow

"Sara?"

Sara yawned and half hiccupped.

And then she realized that she'd been crying and remembered why. She wriggled out of the comforter and sat up blearily. "Hi, Grandpa."

"Are you all right?" Grandpa asked her anxiously.

Sara sniffed and nodded sadly. She was, just about. She was still miserable, but she didn't want to cry anymore.

"You've been asleep a long time, and your mom's on the phone." Grandpa passed it to her. "Come down when you've finished talking to her, all right?"

Sara nodded again. "Hi, Mom," she said huskily.

"Oh, Sara. You sound awful."

"You don't sound very happy, either,"

Sara laughed sadly.

Mom sighed. "Silly, aren't we? Your grandpa said he explained that you're going to have to stay there for now. He doesn't think the snow is going to thaw out anytime soon."

Sara shook her head, and then remembered her mom couldn't see her, and whispered, "No."

"But try not to get upset. We'll wait and have Christmas with you, Sara. We'll put it off until you're back. I'll make your dad eat pasta and salad on Christmas Day."

Sara giggled. "That's mean!"

"Maybe sausage and peppers, then. Oh, sweetheart, I really miss you! Promise me you'll try and enjoy the snow with your grandpa. He says he'll get you home as soon as it's safe. But I wouldn't want him to do anything silly."

"Is it snowy there, too?"

"A little, but nothing like what you've got. I'd better go, sweetheart; I have to see the midwife. I just wanted to call and say hello."

"Thanks," Sara sniffed. "I hope it goes okay. Love you, Mom…."

"Love you, too."

Sara pressed the end call button and sniffed hard a couple more times, trying not to start crying again. It helped that Mom hated it when Sara sniffed—she always told her to blow her nose. Sara could just about manage to laugh at that.

She still felt sad as she walked downstairs and put the phone back in its cradle in Grandpa's study.

He popped out of the kitchen, eyeing her

anxiously. "Are you feeling any better?"

"Mm-hm. Mom says she's going to save Christmas until I'm there, if she has to."

"What about something to eat? You missed lunch. Sandwich?"

Sara shook her head. She wasn't hungry at all. She didn't really know what to do with herself—she'd promised Mom she wouldn't be miserable, but it wasn't easy. In the end, she got a book and curled up on the big couch in the study, watching Grandpa work and trying to read. She didn't get very far. Most of the time she just stared at the strange things all over the walls. They were covered in photographs of her grandpa and great-grandpa on their travels, and the things they'd brought back, like the ivory knife. There was even a canoe hanging from the ceiling.

Sara only picked at her dinner—even though Grandpa had made her favorite, macaroni and cheese. Then she went to bed early, but she couldn't sleep—she'd slept too much earlier in the day, and now she felt jumpy and tired at the same time. In the end she got out of bed and sat on the wide windowsill, staring into the yard.

The igloo was glowing in the winter moonlight, and Sara smiled sadly. It was finished—Grandpa must have finished it for her while she was asleep. The entrance was an arch, and at the back of the igloo she could just about see that he had made her a window—he must have found some ice.

Her snow bear looked strangely real, sitting by the igloo with his big paws dangling sleepily in front of him. Sara wondered if he would move if she sat still and watched for long enough. Then she shook her head angrily. Now she was just being silly. She'd go downstairs and get a drink, she decided. Some warm milk. Maybe that would help her sleep. She padded down the stairs and into the kitchen, glad she'd put her robe on. It was freezing.

Grandpa was standing by the kettle, making himself a hot drink. "You can't sleep, either?"

Sara shook her head. "I was sitting by my window, looking at the snow bear and the igloo," she said.

"What if I told you another story?" Grandpa suggested.

Sara nodded, and then glanced up at him hopefully. "Would you tell it to me in the igloo? I haven't been in it yet—you finished it, and it looks so beautiful."

"You don't mind that I did? I thought it might cheer you up."

"It has." Sara leaned her head against his arm. "And it looks perfect for telling stories in."

Grandpa sighed. "It'll be too cold, Sara! What would your mom say?" He gave her a sudden, worried look, as though he thought he shouldn't have mentioned her mom. "But I guess if we put on our warmest things—and took sleeping bags, and a blanket to sit on...."

"Yes!" Sara hugged him. "And can we have cookies? For a midnight snack in the snow?"

Grandpa rolled his eyes. "Go on, then. I'll make some sandwiches, too."

Sara nudged him. "Tuna fish sandwiches?" Grandpa always had tuna fish sandwiches—they were his favorite, and now Sara loved them, too.

"Mm-hm. Go and get the sleeping bags out of the closet...."

Sara lay snuggled in her sleeping bag, watching the stars tangled in the snowy branches of Grandpa's apple trees. The igloo wasn't big enough for Grandpa to lie down in, but Sara could, if she curled up a little. And the wide arch of the entrance framed the sky, perfect for stargazing. *Mom can see those same stars at home*, Sara thought, blinking sleepily. Mom loved to sit in their screened-in back porch and look up at the stars, even in winter, when the room was freezing. Sara was suddenly sure that her mom was there at that very moment. She found it really hard to sleep, now that she was older, and it wasn't all that late. Only about 11:00.

Sara smiled. It was the nicest thought she'd had since Grandpa had broken the news.

"What are you smiling about?" Grandpa nudged her gently.

"That Mom's probably watching these stars, too, from the back porch. Right now." Sara gave a satisfied little sigh.

Grandpa nodded. "You're probably right. They're amazing, aren't they? Always the same. On and on, forever and ever. Or it seems that way to us, at least. I was looking at these same stars with Alignak and Peter 60 years ago...."

"Tell me the story," Sara said, wriggling closer in her sleeping bag so that she could lean up against him. "The way you always start it...."

Grandpa wrapped his arms around her. "All right." He gave a little cough, clearing his throat, like a real storyteller. "Once upon a time, during the Arctic spring, when there was snow and ice all around, and the days were starting to get longer...."

Sara sighed happily and closed her eyes to listen. That was just right—the proper beginning to the story. Grandpa's voice rumbled, wrapping around her and warming her, the same way his arms did. And the story went on....

CHAPTER SIX

A New Friend

Sara blinked sleepily and gazed out of the arched entrance of the igloo into the strange, purplish light. She hadn't meant to fall asleep, and it was colder than ever. She looked around for Grandpa, thinking that he must have fallen asleep, too, but he wasn't there. Sara struggled up out of her sleeping bag and pulled her boots back on, meaning to hurry into the house and find him.

But as she sat there, tugging at her boots, Sara realized that everything had changed. She hadn't slept in the igloo all night—Grandpa would never have let her. So how could it be light? Or almost light, anyway. The snow around her igloo was glimmering in the light of an odd, pink-streaked sky, as though it was early morning.

The house was gone. They'd built the igloo facing the house—she knew they had. But it wasn't there anymore—and neither was her snow bear. Her boots on at last, Sara crawled out of the igloo and stood up. She stared around, eyes wide.

She wasn't in Grandpa's yard at all.

Snow stretched around her for as far as she could see. There were no houses, not even any trees, just mounds and mountains of snow, with here and there a patch of rock or grass showing through. Sara looked back at her igloo. It was definitely still there, and so was her sleeping bag, and the bag of sandwiches and chocolate cookies. But her snow bear was gone, which just made everything seem even stranger.

She was dreaming. She had to be.

But it was strange to be in a dream and *know* that it was a dream. Tugging her coat more tightly around her shoulders, Sara stepped out into the snow, shivering a little. It was the coldest dream she had ever been in, too.

She looked around, wondering if there was anyone to talk to, to tell her where she was, and called, "Hello…." She didn't call very loudly. She felt shy, somehow, shouting into all that whiteness. And only the wind answered her.

Sara took a few steps around the side of the igloo. She had some odd idea that on the other side of the snow house she might find the way home, that there might be a sort of door back to Grandpa's yard. But she forgot all about that when she came around the back of the igloo and found her snow bear.

He was standing now, on all four paws, but he still only came halfway up Sara's legs. He stared at her uncertainly, with round dark eyes—not green glass anymore—and Sara stared back. His eyes had changed, but it was her bear. She knew it. She knew *him*.

He was *real*—soft and furry. She wanted desperately to pet him, because he looked so much like her cuddly polar bears back home. But this was a real bear now, a wild bear. Sara shook her head, wondering how this could possibly have happened. Then she smiled to herself. She didn't understand it at all, but she'd heard so many of Grandpa's stories, and wished and wished she could see the places he talked about. And now she was in the Arctic!

The cub was looking at her, as though he didn't know what she was, Sara thought. He might never have seen a human before. She looked around anxiously. The bear cub was small—she wasn't really sure how old—but she guessed he was probably only a few months old. So he shouldn't be on his own. Somewhere close by, there would be an enormous mother polar bear, looking for her baby.

Even though Sara thought polar bears were beautiful, she knew how fierce they could be. She watched nature programs about bears, and she had books about them, and Grandpa had told her a ton of stories. They lived mostly by hunting seals, but polar bears could hurt people, too, when they found hunters on their own, or if they thought humans were attacking their cubs. Her little igloo wouldn't be much protection against an angry polar bear.

Sara started to back away slowly, wondering where the mother bear was. She thought it was probably better not to run—polar bears were much faster than people, she was sure. But the polar bear cub gazed after her anxiously, and then took a couple of little steps toward her.

Sara stopped, biting her lip. Was he lost? She was sure that a cub wouldn't usually be away from his mother like this.

The cub ventured closer and gave a whine, a tiny noise that sounded more like a puppy than anything Sara had expected from a bear. She couldn't leave him, she realized. He was too little, and he was scared. She had to help him, somehow. Which was silly, because she thought he probably knew a lot more about surviving in the Arctic than she did.

"Do you need me to help you find your mother?" she said gently, coming a little closer.

The bear looked up at her hopefully, and she sighed. "I don't know where she is. I don't even know where I am, actually. But that must be why I'm here, in this dream, if that's what it is. To take you home."

Sara walked slowly and carefully back to the igloo. The little bear looked hungry, she thought, and she had her sandwiches. She had a feeling he was too young to be eating mostly seal meat, like an adult bear. He was still supposed to be feeding from his mother. But in the Arctic cold, he needed to be fed, even if that meant eating tuna fish sandwiches. Otherwise, he wouldn't have the strength to go far.

"Bet you've never had anything like this," Sara muttered, undoing the foil Grandpa had wrapped around the sandwiches. "I guess it's lucky they're tuna. I don't think you'd like cheese and ketchup—that's my other favorite."

Even though the bear surely hadn't

heard the crinkle of silver foil before, he seemed to know at once that it meant food. He padded over the snow toward Sara and stopped just a step away, looking hopefully from Sara to the foil and back again.

Sara laughed, and then felt guilty as he skittered away. "I'm sorry! I didn't mean to scare you," she whispered. "Yes, they're for you. That's why I opened them. Come on, come and try. You'll like it. Tuna fish is yummy."

The bear sniffed hopefully and looked around, as though he thought he probably shouldn't be doing this, and his mom might suddenly show up and scold him. But when Sara tore off a little piece of sandwich and held it out, he couldn't resist. He snatched it out of her fingers and gulped it down greedily. Then he came closer, looking for more.

"I told you you'd like it," Sara said, feeling happy. "You'd better not have too much, since you're not used to this kind of food. Oh...."

The bear didn't agree. He barged close in to Sara, nudging eagerly at the foil, and rooted around in it.

"Okay, okay. You're really hungry. I know. Here, look, have some more." Sara looked at him worriedly as he gobbled the sandwiches. "I wonder how long you've been on your own. You're still plump, so you probably haven't been hungry for all that long…."

Gently, while he was still eating, she slipped off one glove and rubbed the back of his neck. She was prepared to pull her hand back quickly in case he didn't like it, but he didn't seem to mind. He just glanced at her quickly, checking to see what she was doing, and then went back to the food.

"We'd better find your mother fast," Sara said, sitting down and rubbing the soft folds of fur around his neck. "I just have Grandpa's sandwiches now, and after that it's only chocolate cookies left. I don't think I can give you those. They're probably really bad for you. I know chocolate is bad for dogs. I bet it's not good for bears, either." She shivered. She shouldn't have taken her glove off, but she'd so wanted to feel his fur. Her hand was aching with the cold now, and she felt shivery.

She put the glove back on and carefully patted the bear, rubbing behind his ears and tickling him under the chin, like she tried to do with Iknik. The bear was a lot friendlier, especially now that she'd fed him. He licked all around his jaws—Sara got a glimpse of his teeth, which were very big, even though he wasn't—and he sniffed her gloves to see if she was bringing more food.

"I need to give you a name," Sara said thoughtfully. "I can't just call you bear." She ran her hand over his domed white head, and the bear nuzzled at her wrist. "Oh! Of course." She smiled. "I'll call you Peter. Like Grandpa's bear." She shook her head, suddenly confused. "Maybe you *are* Grandpa's bear! Maybe I'm taking you back to your mother, so the boys don't have to leave you on the sea-ice at the end of the summer!" Sara frowned. "But that would be silly. How can I be inside Grandpa's story? And it's not a dream, I'm sure it's not. You're real. I can feel you. You can't feel things the same way in dreams...."

She stood up, looking around anxiously. How was she going to find a white bear in all this snow? "Maybe you can find her," she suggested to Peter. "Polar bears hunt by smell, I'm sure I read that. Can you follow your mother's scent? Can you track her? Or maybe you're just too little."

Peter stood next to her, very close, his soft head almost resting on the side of her coat, so that she could feel the warmth of him. Sara thought that he seemed to be waiting for her to tell him what to do. He was used to following his mother.

"I wish we had some idea where to go," Sara muttered. "What if I head in the wrong direction, and just take you farther away from her?"

Peter put his nose down and snuffled thoughtfully at the snow, looking up at Sara with dark, sparkling eyes.

"What is it?" She bent down to look and took in a quick, excited breath. "Tracks!

Aren't you clever!" The tracks were hard to see—she'd never have seen them herself—but they were definitely there. And they were too big to be Peter's own paw prints—they were big, heavy pads pressed into the loose snow, setting off across the whiteness, like a trail to follow. "She must have lost you, somehow, and gone off looking for you. We just have to catch up to her," Sara said firmly. She picked up the little bag of sandwiches and cookies and started to follow the prints of the big-footed bear, leading the cub out into the snow.

CHAPTER
SEVEN

Looking for a Bear

Sara and the bear followed the tracks. It was a strange way to walk, eyes down, peering at the faint paw prints. Every so often, they seemed to fade away, as though fresh snow had fallen over them, and Sara was worried that they would lose the trail. But each time, Peter would sniff around and come across the tracks again.

Sara pulled the hood of her coat up around her ears, wishing that she'd put more sweaters on underneath. She'd thought it was cold at Grandpa's, but it was nothing like this. She pressed closer to the bear cub, feeling the warmth of his fur under her gloved hand as they walked on.

The white landscape was very quiet, and at first Sara thought it was empty. But then Peter stopped in surprise as a white creature raced over the snow in front of them, stopped for a second to look, and dashed away as the bear cub made a strange, angry grunting sound.

Sara gazed after it, trying to see what it was as it skipped from patches of snow to the darker tundra that was showing through. It looked like a big, old-fashioned powder puff, with a pair of long, dark-tipped ears. "An Arctic hare," Sara said as it disappeared into the distance. The dark eyes and nose looked like pebbles against the snow, and the hare blurred as it ran—its camouflage was perfect. She remembered seeing a photo of a hare in one of the books she'd read about polar bears. But there hardly seemed to be enough green stuff around for it to eat. Just mossy patches here and there.

"It would help if you could eat this, too," she said to Peter, crouching down to look at the yellowish lichen. "I think I'd better save the second bag of sandwiches a little longer, just in case."

The polar bear cub sniffed at the lichen and looked up at her so disgustedly that she had to laugh. "I don't think I'd like it, either," she admitted. Then she shivered again. Was it really getting colder? She wasn't certain what time of year it was here—she was pretty sure the Arctic would be completely covered in snow in winter, which meant this had to be spring or summer. But it was so cold, and it was starting to snow again, she realized in dismay, watching the snowflakes start to float gently down. They were so pretty and delicate—but there were so many of them, and they were falling faster and faster. Sara took a sudden tight grip on Peter's fur. She could hardly see him now, a white bear in a white whirling snowstorm.

"It's a blizzard," she whispered, the

cold stealing her voice away. "We can't stay out in this. We'll freeze...."

Peter tugged at her hand and she gasped, frightened that he'd run off, and she would lose him. But he looked back up at her, his dark eyes glinting among the snowflakes. He wanted her to follow him.

Step by step, half blind, Sara followed the little bear to a strange cave, a dark hole in a snowdrift that appeared suddenly out of the storm. Peter dived inside and then turned around, seizing Sara's coat in his sharp little teeth, and dragging her after him. Sitting down inside the earthy burrow, away from the biting wind, Sara gasped, trying to catch her breath. The cold seemed to have frozen her lungs. Peter snuggled up next to her and sniffed hopefully at the bag of sandwiches. Sara fumbled at it and tore off a little piece of sandwich for herself, feeding the rest to the bear cub. Then Peter curled up half across her lap and nudged her lovingly before he fell asleep.

Sara stared out at the dark snowstorm, wondering what they were going to do now. Maybe another one of these sudden blizzards had blown up before, and that was how Peter had been separated from his mother.

The cub sighed in his sleep, and Sara rubbed his white fur—he was almost as fluffy as that powderpuff of a hare. He was so young, and he trusted her. She had to get him back to his mother. But as Sara gazed out into the storm, she knew that all his mother's footprints would have been covered long ago....

Sara fell asleep, too, eventually—the flickering fall of the snowflakes was hard to watch without her eyelids starting to close. When she woke up, it had stopped snowing, and the landscape stretched out into whiteness in front of her.

Peter woke, wriggling, and bounced over to the little tunnel's entrance hole, peering out at the snow eagerly. *Maybe he's hoping to see his mother*, Sara thought sadly, watching him stick his head out.

She blinked, suddenly realizing where they must be. This was a maternity den, where a mother polar bear had hidden herself over the winter, digging down through a snowdrift to the earth below, to make a safe nest for herself and her babies. It was probably where Peter had been born. He must have sniffed it out, catching his mother's scent in the storm. Maybe he'd been heading to the den when Sara found him.

Sara followed him out into the snow, looking around hopefully for the paw prints. She knew they must have been covered up, but still…. Peter sniffed at the fresh snow, looking up at her in confusion.

"I know," Sara muttered. "We'll just have to find your mother another way. It'll be all right."

The little bear ran off into the snow, kicking up the fresh powder with his claws and squeaking. Sara giggled. Even though she was worried, she couldn't not laugh—he was so funny, dancing around in the snow. He didn't seem to feel the cold as much as she did. *His fur is perfectly designed for the Arctic weather,* Sara thought to herself. She couldn't even feel her fingers anymore. She shook her head, as if it might help her feel less dopey with the cold.

Peter stopped sharply and gave a little growl, staring down at the ground. He'd found something. Sara hurried over to him, clapping her hands together to try to warm them up.

Tracks. But not bear tracks—these were long, thin grooves, with smaller paw prints here and there. A dog sled. Sara felt her heart jump with excitement—they weren't alone in the snow, as she'd thought. Maybe whoever had driven past in the sled would have seen Peter's mother and would be able to tell her where to take him.

They set off again, following the sled tracks this time. The sled must have passed by their den since the snow stopped falling, Sara realized. It couldn't be that far ahead of them, although it would be moving much faster than they were. There was still a chance they could catch up. Maybe the sled might stop for the dogs to rest. If only she could keep walking. She was so tired, even though they must have slept for a long time in the den, and it seemed like such an effort just to lift her feet. Peter was tiring quickly, too. He'd slowed down, and he kept looking up at her hopefully and nudging at the food bag with his nose.

"No more sandwiches," Sara told him apologetically. "Maybe if we catch up with the sled, whoever's driving it will have something for you." Then she stopped, staring out across the snow, her heart racing.

That noise—a low, mournful howling. She'd heard it before, but only in movies, never for real. It was a noise from the kind of movies where she liked to hide behind her mom on the couch, with her dad teasing them about being scared.

It was a wolf.

Peter gave her a frightened look and darted sideways.

If he was with his mother, Sara thought, *he'd be fine.* She'd scare the wolves away. Sara had only heard one howling, but it wouldn't be alone. Wolves traveled in packs. They wouldn't attack an adult bear, especially one with a cub to protect—she would be too fierce, and it would be too risky. But a girl and a bear cub—they were easy prey. Sara didn't have any way to fight back—not even with Grandpa's ivory knife. Had the wolves caught their scent? The noise seemed to be coming from a distance. Maybe if they were lucky....

The howling came again, and Sara realized with dismay that it was in front of them—on the same course as the tracks. To stay away from the wolves, they'd have to move away from the tracks and lose their chance of catching up with the sled.

But they didn't have a choice.

CHAPTER EIGHT

A Helping Hand

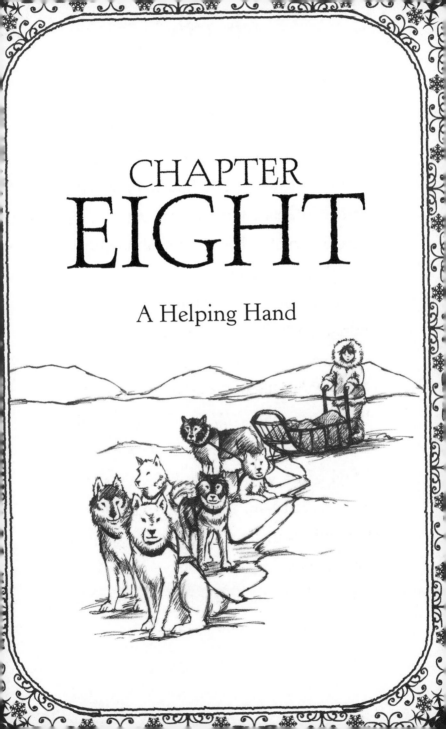

They hurried on, striking out sideways from the tracks, Sara hoping that it would take them away from the wolves. The howling seemed a little fainter and farther away. At least the scare had woken her up a bit, although she wasn't any warmer.

Peter was whimpering now, tired and hungry, and Sara stopped to pet him and whisper in his ears. "We have to keep going. What about those wolves? We can't let them catch us. We're doing the right thing, Peter. I can't hear them anymore. Maybe in a while we'll come across the sled tracks again...." But she wasn't very hopeful about that. They'd gone too far out of their way. She'd have to look for a town instead, or another hunter. She couldn't give up. She wouldn't.

Eventually Peter simply stopped, shaking his head like a sulky child, refusing to go any further.

Sara looked at him anxiously. "What's the matter? Are you hurt? Come on, little bear. We can't just stop. We'll both freeze."

But Peter stayed where he was, his paws planted stubbornly in the snow, shaking his head, and making that odd chuffing little growl again.

Sara sighed. Maybe he'd follow her if she went on a bit. He was tired, that was all. She took a few steps away from him, hoping he'd stop being grouchy and catch up to her. She turned back to see if he was going to follow and smiled as she saw him start to run forward. It was working!

Her sigh of relief turned to surprise as Peter yipped worriedly and caught her pant leg in his teeth—but too late. She was already falling. A crevasse in the ice had opened up beneath her, and she hadn't even seen it. *Peter must have known,* she thought wearily. She seemed to be turning over and over as she tumbled into the darkness, and everything was horribly slow. *He sensed something was wrong. He wasn't being sulky. He was trying to stop me. I should have realized....*

Her head hurt. Sara tried to sit up, but that only made her feel sick and dizzy, and when she opened her eyes, everything went white.

She blinked.

Actually, everything *was* white. She'd forgotten for a moment, that was all. She was in some strange world of dream and snow, trying to return a lost polar bear cub to his mother. And now she had fallen into a crevasse, a great tear in the ice. How far down was she?

She peered up again, more carefully this time, trying not to jar her aching head. Peter was looking down at her, a white furry head leaning over the edge of the icy cliff, eyeing her worriedly.

He was a long way up. Maybe an arm's length farther than she could reach. She couldn't get back up there, not without a rope, and someone to pull. The ice looked sheer—there were no useful little footholds to climb up by. She wasn't sure she could climb even if there were—she felt all wobbly.

Peter whined worriedly, and Sara tried to stand up to tell him it was all right. But she had a horrible feeling it wasn't. She was stuck.

She blinked again. There was another face now, another furry face, staring down at her over the lip of the crevasse. She squinted, half closing her eyes against the low sunlight, and realized that it was a boy wearing a fur-trimmed hood. An Inuit boy, a few years older than her.

Peter had edged away from him, but he
was still there.

"Did you fall down?" the boy called.

Sara nodded and wished she hadn't.
"Yes," she whispered, wincing. It was a
silly question, anyway. What did he think
had happened?

"All right. Don't worry. I just need to undo some of the harness, then I can use it to pull you out."

"Thank you...," Sara said quietly, wrapping her arms around her middle. It was even colder down in the crevasse, although at least she was sheltered from the wind. She could hear it whining and whistling as it blew over the top of the huge crack in the ice.

What did the boy mean, harness? She thought of calling back to ask but didn't. She didn't want to slow him down.

"Can you tie this around yourself?" A strip of dark stuff that looked like oiled leather was dangling above her, and the boy's face was staring down at her. She could see his mittened hand, too, guiding the harness so it fell toward her.

Of course. It was his sled they'd followed, and those strange whining noises weren't just the wind. There was a team of sled dogs up there, and he'd unfastened their harness so he could use it to pull her out. They must have wandered close to the sled tracks again after all. Sara tied the harness around her waist and held on to it as tightly as she could. She wasn't sure how the boy was going to pull her out. He looked bigger than she was, but not that much bigger. Surely she would be too heavy for him to manage on his own....

"Hold on! We'll start pulling you up now," he called down to her, and Sara gasped as the harness tightened, and she started to bump slowly up the icy wall. He was using the dogs to help him drag her up—she could hear their claws scuffling on the ice, and their confused whining as they pulled this strange load.

The ice wasn't quite as smooth as it had looked from down below, and Sara was able to push herself up a little by digging her toes into the cracks here and there. But it was still a slow and difficult climb, and she was exhausted by the time the boy hauled her over the lip of the crevasse.

"Thank you!" she gasped, and then let out a breathless laugh as Peter hurled himself at her, nuzzling her anxiously. He kept sniffing and nudging at her, obviously trying to make sure she was all right.

"So he's yours? You've got a polar bear cub?" the boy asked her curiously as he untied the harness and fixed it back on to the sled with the six dogs jumping around him excitedly. "How did you find him?"

Sara shook her head very carefully. Her headache wasn't as bad as it had been before, but it was still definitely there. She must have hit her head as she fell. "He found me," she told the boy. "He's lost. I was trying to help him find his mother, but the snowstorm covered her tracks." She staggered, almost falling, and the boy grabbed her arms.

"You look frozen. Here, sit down on the sled. Wrap these around you." He half led, half pushed her to the dog-sled, grabbing a bundle of soft, grayish furs that Sara thought were probably seal skin. She felt sorry for the seals, but they were incredibly warm!

"That's better." The boy nodded approvingly. "You're lucky I saw your bear cub. There's a wolf pack close—I heard them howling."

"We heard them, too," Sara whispered, huddling herself into the furs.

"Eat some of this." The boy undid one of the packages tied to the sled. "You need to keep eating out here. You have to keep your strength up in the cold."

Sara looked at the strange, leathery stuff he was trying to feed her and nibbled a little bit of it politely. It was horrible. It tasted fishy and oily and dry, all at the same time. She guessed it was some kind of preserved fish. She burrowed under the seal skins for the bag of food she'd brought from home and pulled out two chocolate cookies. She handed one to the boy, and he looked at it as though he'd never seen anything like it before. "Maybe you've never had chocolate. You'll love it. Oh, my head hurts...."

The boy was looking at her worriedly, but he was eating the cookie and obviously liked it. Sara sneaked her piece of dried fish to Peter, who she'd pulled up next to her on the sled. He needed it more than she did, she told herself, feeling a little bit guilty. Peter didn't seem to mind the taste at all, and he snuggled up next to her under the seal skins, casting nervous glances at the dogs. They were a little bigger than he was, and very loud. The boy had fastened their harnesses back on, but they weren't lined up in pairs, the way Sara had expected. Instead, they were harnessed in a sort of fan shape in front of the sled. They kept turning around and staring at Sara and Peter with bright, inquisitive eyes.

Sara looked at the boy, licking chocolate from around his lips eagerly. He seemed familiar, somehow. But she couldn't figure out why. Her sore head was making everything seem strange, and it was only as the boy climbed onto the sled in front of her and called to the dogs, sending them racing over the snow, that Sara wondered how she could understand what he was saying. She'd been talking to him all this time, and she was sure they weren't speaking English.

CHAPTER
NINE

Introducing Alignak

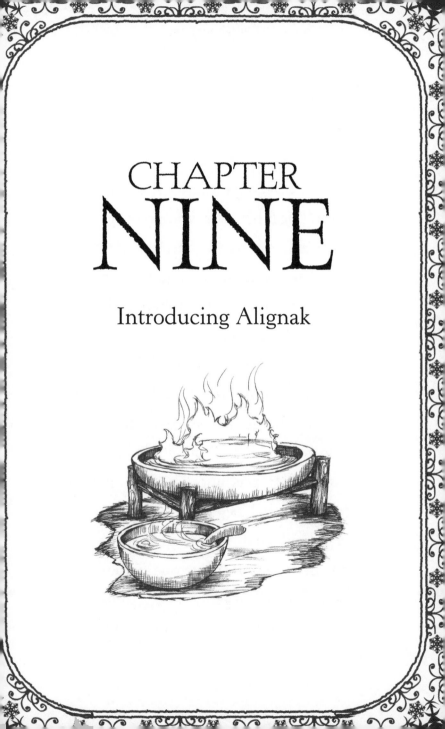

Sara was about to ask the boy who he was, but with the wind whistling around them, and the snow crunching under the sled runners, she knew he wouldn't hear her. She wrapped herself up in the furs more tightly and leaned against Peter. Now that she was getting warmer again, her fingers throbbed painfully inside her fleece gloves.

Where was he taking them? Somewhere warm, hopefully. He'd said she looked cold. She stared ahead, over the backs of the racing dogs, but all she saw was whiteness. It was another half an hour before the sled began to slow, and she understood that the smooth hump of snow in front of them was actually an igloo. A real, large igloo, nothing like the little one she and Grandpa had built. She gazed at it admiringly as they pulled up by the side, and the sled dogs immediately started barking excitedly.

This igloo had an entrance tunnel, half buried in the snow. The igloo was taller than Sara was—she guessed it was about the same height as her grandpa, maybe a little taller. It was built of huge blocks of snow, each about a foot and a half long, and fit together perfectly. It shone in the pinkish light, and Sara smiled at the sight of it. She hadn't ever thought that an igloo could be so beautiful.

The boy sprang down from the sled and started to unharness the dogs and fasten them to posts dug into the snow. He saw that Sara was watching him questioningly. "They sleep outdoors."

"Won't they be cold?" Sara asked,

looking at the dogs anxiously.

But the boy only laughed and pointed to the nearest dog, who was curled up in the snow, with his tail wrapped tightly around his nose and his paws. Sara had never seen a dog curl up so small—he looked almost like a cat. "They can sleep through a blizzard like that. And they have to stay out—they're our guard dogs, too. They let us know if there's a polar bear around."

Sara hugged Peter tightly. "They won't hurt him, will they?"

The boy shook his head. "No, I don't think so. He's too little. And maybe he smells like you."

The boy finished tying up the dogs and came toward her, holding out a hand to help her off the sled. "You'd better come in. You need to eat. My grandmother will make you some soup—that'll warm you up. My father still isn't back with a seal, and you look too cold to wait." He hauled her off the sled, and Peter leaped off after her. Then the boy ducked down, stooping into the entrance of the igloo, and waving at her to follow him.

Sara laid her hand on Peter's neck, calling him to follow, but he wasn't sure about going into the little tunnel. Maybe the igloo smelled strangely of humans. He sniffed at it doubtfully and looked up at her. Then at last he gave himself a little shake, as though he'd decided it must be all right if she was going in. Together, they crept inside the snow house.

As Sara emerged into the main room of the igloo, blinking in the dim light, the boy seemed to be arguing with someone.

"You see! I'm sorry I didn't bring back any fish, but I'm not telling a story. I did find a girl," the boy said triumphantly, coming to pull her farther in. "She'd fallen into a crevasse. I saw the bear cub first. I wanted to know why he was staring over the edge of the ice like that." Proudly, he turned Sara to face an elderly lady, sitting on a pile of skins spread over a ledge of snow that ran across the far side of the igloo. She was wrapped in skins, too, with a kind of furry poncho over a bright fringed and embroidered tunic, and a pair of the same soft furry boots that the boy was wearing. She was sitting by a strange bowl-shaped lamp full of oil and sewing by the light it gave her.

The elderly lady shook her head. "A girl and a bear. Like one of the old tales, Alignak. You're right, though—I could have done with those fish." She turned to Sara. "Where have you come from, child? And who sent you out dressed like that? You look half frozen." Frowning, she tugged at Sara's coat sleeve as though she didn't approve of it at all. "Come here and sit by the *qulliq*. Maybe you came from the lights," she whispered. "One of the ancestors, come down from the sky...."

"It feels warm in here," Sara said as she sat where the elderly lady showed her, holding out her hands over the stone oil lamp. Grandpa had talked about lamps like this, hadn't he? That they melted the inside of the igloo? She looked up at the snow wall and saw that it was a sheet of smooth ice, like he'd said. But she hadn't expected the igloo to feel so cozy when it was made of snow! There was even a block of greenish ice, halfway up the wall, for a window.

The elderly lady bustled around, finding some more dried meat and putting it into a small stone pot that she balanced on a frame over the lamp. "Go and get me some snow, Alignak," she told the boy. "I'll make some broth to warm her up." Then she eyed Peter thoughtfully. "I have no fresh seal meat for you, little one, not until my son and Alignak's brother come back from hunting. You'll have to eat the dried caribou, like your girl." She cut off a strip and fed it to Peter, who was lying across Sara's feet. She was actually starting to be able to feel her toes again, and she was thinking more clearly in the warmth. Who did Alignak and his grandmother think she was?

And who were they?

Then she remembered. That was where she knew him from! The photograph!

Alignak was the boy her grandpa had known, she was sure. The boy who'd been with him when he found the bear cub. It was as though she was inside her favorite story. Sara shook her head. She didn't understand, and she didn't think Alignak and his grandmother did, either. But maybe it didn't really matter. The important thing was to find Peter's mother and make sure he was safe. Sara sat watching the orange flames flickering on the oil lamp and feeling Peter shift and wriggle on her feet as he gnawed at the dried meat.

The broth in the stone pot was starting to steam gently. It smelled like the tins of beef and vegetable soup her dad liked to have when it was cold. Sara bit her lip. She didn't want to think about home—it was too far away—but it was hard not to. Dad might be having soup for lunch, too.

"Here." Alignak's grandmother passed

her a wide ivory spoon and beckoned her to sit by the cooking pot. "This should warm you up."

Sara sipped the broth, blowing on it, and wincing as it burned her lips. After the dried fish, she hadn't been sure she'd like the soup, but it was hot and delicious, and soon she could feel the warmth spreading through her. She offered the spoon to Alignak, but he shook his head.

"No, you eat it. My father and brother will be back soon with a seal."

While Sara was eating, the elderly lady was searching through a pile of clothes, glancing over at Sara, and muttering to herself. She turned over soft furs, and more of the beautiful embroidered tunics that she was wearing. Sara had seen photos of Inuit people dressed in clothes like these back at Grandpa's, but they'd all been in black-and-white. She hadn't expected the clothes to be so brightly colored.

As soon as Sara had finished the soup, Alignak's grandmother held up a pair of mittens and a hood and nodded. "These should fit. Take off those other ones— they're no use at all."

Sara obediently slipped her fleece gloves into her pockets and put the fur mittens on.

"They're caribou skin," Alignak told her. "Much warmer than yours. Caribou makes the best snow clothes."

Sara nodded. The mittens felt warm and soft. The Inuit people used every part of the animals they hunted, Grandpa had told her, even the stomach and other insides. Nothing was wasted. She might

not have wanted to wear fur at home, but
here, in this strange snowy dream, she
knew she needed the mittens. The elderly
lady tied the hood around her chin and
looked pleased.

"Thank you," Sara whispered, reaching down to pet Peter, who was pulling at her leg with his teeth.

"He wants to go," Alignak said, and Sara nodded.

"But we don't know where we're going," she sighed. "The storm buried his mother's tracks. How am I supposed to find her?"

Alignak frowned. "She'll be farther out on the sea ice, where the seals come up," he told her, glancing at his grandmother, who nodded. "Hunting. There's a lead, not too far from here, where we often see bears."

Sara shook her head apologetically. "What's a *lead*?"

The boy blinked as though he couldn't believe she didn't know. "Open water—

like a channel in the ice. Bears like to hunt there. We hunt there, too, sometimes. I can show you which way to go...." He looked as though he'd like to go, too, but his grandmother was shaking her head.

She probably doesn't want him to get gobbled up by an angry mother polar bear, Sara thought to herself, shivering a little, even with the warm mittens and hood. *Or maybe she thinks I'm some kind of strange creature out of an old story.*

"You should wait for my son to come back," the elderly lady said firmly. "Alignak's father. He'll take you—that will be safer."

But Peter was pulling at her leg again and making anxious little growling noises. He seemed determined that they go now. Sara smiled gratefully at Alignak and his grandmother. "I can't wait—it's starting to get dark, isn't it? I'll have no chance of finding Peter's mother then."

She didn't want to say it, but if she waited for the hunters to get back and take her to the lead, they would probably frighten the mother bear away. Or worse, she might know what hunters looked like and decide to attack them. It was safer for everyone if she and Peter went by themselves.

"Thank you for the soup, and for feeding Peter," she told the elderly lady. "It was very kind of you."

"We always share what we have," Alignak said, sounding almost surprised. "Food belongs to everyone who needs it. Come on. I'll take you toward the break in the sea ice—just a little way," he added to his grandmother, who nodded reluctantly.

"I wish I could come with you all the way," Alignak said as they came out into the snow again, and he led her toward the ice hills behind the igloo. "But the bears—it's too dangerous, unless we're in a hunting party." He looked at her worriedly and caught her hand, as though he wanted to pull her back to the safety of the igloo. "I have to go back. Will you really be all right?"

Sara swallowed and nodded firmly. "Yes." She was fairly sure she couldn't be eaten in a story. Almost sure, anyway. She hugged Alignak, surprised at how small he felt under his layers of furs, and laughed at his shocked face. "Good-bye!" she called as she walked away, turning back every so often to wave. Peter galloped ahead of her, full of energy now that he'd eaten.

The last time she turned back, Alignak and the igloo seemed to have melted away, settling back into the snowy whiteness, as if they had never been there at all.

CHAPTER TEN

Reunited

Had it only been a trick of the fading light? Sara almost ran back to see, but something stopped her. It was better to keep going, and Peter was darting ahead of her. She hurried after the little bear— she couldn't risk losing him.

To get to the lead, where Alignak thought Peter's mother might be, they had to walk through a maze of strange ice hills, where the ice had been squashed up over the years until it looked like waves on the ocean. It was hard going, picking her way through the icy hummocks, and Sara's legs were aching. Peter's furry feet and sharp claws were built for scrambling over ice, and he kept bouncing along in front of her, turning back every so often to run around behind and herd her along, like a lost sheep.

"I know. You want to see your mother. Soon. I'm sure we'll find her soon," Sara muttered, stopping to rest for a minute. "I hope so, anyway," she added, glancing anxiously at the sky. It was getting dark, the low sun striking the ice formations and turning them a glowing pink. It was beautiful—but scary. What if they had to spend a night out here on the ice? They could try to find their way back to the igloo, but they'd already been walking for a while, and it would be fully dark before they got back. If the snow house was even still there.

She shivered suddenly as an eerie howl echoed around the snowy hills. The wolves were back. Peter slunk closer to her, pressing anxiously against her legs. *I should have asked Alignak for a bow and arrows*, Sara thought, biting her lip. She wasn't sure how far they were from the lead—Alignak had said it was an hour's walk. It felt like they'd been walking for longer. Maybe they were close. It would be so unfair if the wolves drove them off-course again.

Maybe she could throw a stone—except there weren't any. A chunk of ice? She searched frantically around at her feet, trying to find something, anything, she could use as a weapon.

Then a low, threatening growl made her stop, her breath catching in her throat. Was that the wolves? Were they closer? She stood up slowly, trying to push Peter behind her. Maybe the wolves would be so surprised to see a human they'd run off, especially if she shouted. She couldn't let them hurt the little bear.

But then Peter darted forward, making excited little squeaking noises, and Sara gulped. An enormous polar bear was running toward them, so fast that she was swinging from side to side.

Sara felt her eyes fill with joyful tears,

and she rubbed an icy mitten across her face to brush them away before they froze. They had found her! The huge white bear was Peter's mother. It had to be, from the way he was leaping joyfully around her.

The big bear sniffed him carefully all over, making sure he was all right. Then she nuzzled him lovingly, rubbing her huge head up and down his soft fur again and again. At last, she looked up, staring curiously at Sara. She took a step toward her, and Sara realized that the mother bear's paw prints in the snow made hers look tiny, even though she had her big boots on. Sara had gotten used to thinking of polar bears as Peter-sized. Small and cuddly. This bear was taller on all four paws than Sara was standing up. If the bear stood up on her hind legs to fight, she'd be giant.

Sara swallowed. She wasn't sure if the bear knew what she'd been doing—that she'd been trying to help. What if Peter's mother thought she was dangerous, that Sara was someone who might hurt her baby? She stood still, looking down at her small feet, and trying not to seem scary.

But the bear didn't come any closer. She nudged Peter firmly and turned around, heading back the way she'd come. Peter glanced back at Sara and hesitated but followed his mother. They set off across the snow, leaving Sara all alone.

She'd done it. She'd brought Peter back to his mother.

Sara tried to smile, but she felt too tired and too sad. She'd only known the little bear for a day, but now that he was gone, she felt lost. She sank down slowly, so that she was sitting in the snow. She knew she shouldn't—if she sat down, she'd get too cold. She had to keep moving. She had to find her own way home now.

She'd only sit for a little while. Tears ran slowly down her cheeks, and she felt them freeze. A few snowflakes drifted gently past her.

Then someone nudged her, a gentle push against her shoulder, and Sara looked up slowly.

They were back. Peter's mother was standing over her. So close that Sara could see her eyes, black and glinting and curious. She nudged Sara again, shoving her so that she'd stand up. Sara staggered to her feet obediently, and the bear seemed to be pleased. She crouched down in the snow, stretching her forepaws out in front of her, and pushed Sara up against her side.

Sara looked worriedly at Peter. Did his mother want her to climb onto her back? Peter darted toward her and pushed the back of her knees. Sara did as she was told, clambering onto the huge back, just behind the bear's shoulder. She'd ridden a pony before, but the bear was so big, and so wide. It was like sitting on a couch—a warm, white, slightly smelly couch that moved. Sara gave a squeak as the bear set off, swaying gently as she walked. Peter ran along beside them, looking up at Sara happily, and occasionally dancing off in front of his mother to snap at the snowflakes and scuffle around, just like a little boy.

Sara stared around her. It was almost completely dark, and a light snow was falling. The sky was scattered with stars, and she smiled sadly, remembering the stars in Grandpa's yard and at home. How was she going to get back?

She frowned a little, staring at the sky—a strange, greenish-white band had appeared, stretching across the stars, and as she watched, it grew. The light stretched into a curtain that seemed to be hanging in the sky, rippling and shimmering. Purple streaks danced across it, and Sara laughed in delight.

The polar bear stopped, gazing up at the lights and nuzzling her cub.

"The northern lights," Sara whispered. "Grandpa told me about them. I wish I could go back and tell him I've seen them, too...." She leaned forward, resting her face against the polar bear's fur and looking up at the lights swirling and dancing through the sky. There were pictures in it now.... Two bears, large and small. She laughed again quietly and stretched down one hand to rub Peter's head.

Peter rubbed his muzzle against her hand lovingly and turned back to look at the pictures in the sky.

Sara reached out a hand toward the lights. Her mother's face.... She was smiling....

"Sara?" A deep voice was calling her gently, and Sara blinked, not sure where she was. A moment ago, she'd been lying pillowed against the thick, yellowish-white fur of a polar bear. She sat up a little, shaking her head, and rubbed the fur under her fingers again—the furry lining of her grandpa's hooded coat.

She was back! Back with Grandpa—she was safe!

But it had been a dream, then, she realized miserably. She hadn't saved Peter at all. She'd just woven it out of Grandpa's story, and her own wish to be at home with her mother.

"I didn't mean to let you fall asleep, Sara, love," her grandpa said gently. "I was telling the story and remembering. It all seemed so real again, looking out at the snow. And when I glanced down, you'd drifted off. We'd better go back inside. Get you into your bed."

Sara nodded, standing up, and stretching out her fingers. Same old pink fleece gloves. Not caribou-fur mittens. She supposed they would have been hard to explain at school. She hefted her sleeping bag into her arms and the little packet of sandwiches and smiled sadly up at Grandpa.

"We never ate them."

"Never mind. I'll put them in the fridge. We might need them tomorrow, I think." Grandpa took the bag, nodding mysteriously, but Sara wasn't listening.

"Grandpa, look! My snow bear's gone. He melted away."

There was only a shapeless snowy lump left behind. Sara's eyes filled with tears. Somehow that made it even worse—she didn't even have a snow bear cub anymore. She sniffed and blinked the tears away, and the bright moonlight caught something sparkling in the snow outside the igloo.

Sara reached down and picked up the two pieces of green sea glass that had been her little bear's eyes. They glowed gently, with the soft green of the northern lights. She turned them over in her hand, her eyes widening. They'd changed. The green glow wasn't just the moonlight on the glass. It was *inside*, she was sure. And the glass was a different shape now—both pieces were paw prints, a little paw, and a huge, heavy paw, soft triangles, edged with a ridge of claws.

Sara slipped them into her pocket. "Grandpa? Can I keep the sea glass I used for his eyes?" she asked, smiling to herself.

"Of course you can. I wonder why he melted so much faster than the rest of the snow," Grandad said thoughtfully as they walked toward the house. "I don't think the roads will be clear until tomorrow morning."

Sara shook her head. Then she realized what Grandpa had said and whirled around, dropping her sleeping bag in the snow. "The roads will be clear? Do you really think they will be? You can take me home?"

Grandpa picked it up and put an arm around her. "I think I'd better. Your dad called my cell phone while you were asleep. You need to get home and meet your brother, and I want to spend Christmas with both of my grandchildren." His eyes twinkled.

"Mom had the baby already?" Sara gasped.

"Mm-hm. And they named him Peter." Grandpa smiled at her as they hurried into the warmth of the house. "Just like my polar bear, Sara. I told you it was your dad's favorite story, too." He put down the sleeping bag and took hold of her hands. "You would have loved him, Sara, my little bear. I know it's silly, but I wish you could have met him."

Sara nodded and wrapped her arms around Grandpa's neck.

"I did…," she whispered, very, very quietly.

LEARN MORE ABOUT THE WONDERFUL WINTRY WORLD OF SARA AND HER SNOW BEAR

AMAZING
POLAR BEARS

Polar bears are longer and larger than other bears. Adults can grow to be more than 8 feet (2.5 m) long and weigh around 1,500 pounds (680 kg). They are the biggest living carnivores!

Although they're huge, polar bears are strong swimmers because they have webbed feet. They can swim effortlessly—their back feet act like paddles.

Polar bears live across the Arctic. They can be found in parts of the United States, Canada, Russia, Greenland, and Norway.

Although polar bears' fur looks white, it's actually transparent! It has a hollow core, which reflects light. The skin under their fur is black, which helps them to soak up the sun and stay warm.

When they're born, polar bear cubs are just 12 inches (30 cm) in length and weigh about the same as a guinea pig. They stay with their mother for two years while they learn essential survival skills.

Polar bears need sea ice to hunt seals, which make up 95% of their diet. Global warming means that there is less sea ice, and polar bears have to travel farther to find food.

Polar bears rest for up to 20 hours per day when they aren't hunting.

In order to
survive the harsh
climate of the Arctic,
polar bears have a
thick layer of fat
(blubber) to insulate
them from extremely
cold air and water.

Polar bears don't slip
on the ice because they
have stiff fur on the
soles of their feet. This
also helps them hunt, as
they can approach their
prey almost silently.

The name for
a group of polar
bears is a pack
or a sleuth.

POLAR BEARS AREN'T
THE ONLY AMAZING
ANIMALS YOU'LL MEET
IN THE ARCTIC....

WHO ELSE LIVES IN THE ARCTIC?

ARCTIC WOLVES

These wolves have two layers of fur—the outer layer becomes thicker in the winter, and the inner layer is waterproof. These animals can also withstand up to 5 months of complete darkness each year!

BEARDED SEALS

Bearded seals got their name from their long and elaborate whiskers, which often curl when dry. In the Canadian Arctic, seal pups are born in May and enter the water just hours after being born.

ARCTIC TERN

The arctic tern, also known as a sea swallow, breeds on the Arctic tundra and spends the winter in Antarctica. Arctic terns have the longest migration of any bird— a round trip of up to 22,000 miles every year!

ARCTIC HARES
Arctic hares have thick hair, which help them to survive in their harsh habitat. In winter their fur is white to camouflage with the snow, but in the spring, they are a blue-gray color, which helps them blend in with rocks and vegetation.

ORCAS
Commonly known as killer whales, orcas are actually part of the dolphin family. They are one of the most powerful predators in the world and tend to live for around 50 to 80 years.

GREATER SNOW GEESE
These birds can fly at speeds of 59 miles per hour (95 kph) and fly without stopping for up to 620 miles (1,000 km). At one day old, a snow goose can already walk more than 18 miles (30 km).

SARA'S ADVENTURE
TAKES HER TO THE
CANADIAN ARCTIC.

TURN THE PAGE TO FIND
OUT MORE ABOUT THIS
SNOWY SETTING AND THE
PEOPLE WHO LIVE THERE....

A LAND OF
ICE AND SNOW

* The Canadian Arctic, at the very north of Canada, makes up around 40% of the Canadian landmass.

* North of mainland Canada are 94 major islands that form the Arctic archipelago. There are also 36,469 minor islands!

* The scenery varies in the Canadian Arctic, from mountains to fjords to plains.

* The average daily temperature is -4°F (-20°C) from December to March, and in some places, it's as cold as -58°F (-50°C).

* Nighttime in the winter months lasts for 24 hours in the northern islands, and in the summer, daytime lasts for 24 hours.

* There isn't much rain in the Arctic—around 16 inches (40 cm) per year on the southern islands and as little as 4 inches (10 cm) on the central islands.

* Global warming affects the Arctic at faster rates than other parts of the world, causing increased rainfall, a reduction in sea ice, and glaciers to retreat.

* Polar bears are now classified as vulnerable and are at risk of starving. With less sea ice, polar bears have to travel farther to hunt seals. This extra activity makes them weaker and makes hunting more difficult.

PEOPLE OF THE ARCTIC

Due to the harsh conditions in the Canadian Arctic, the population is only around 100,000. Most of the islands are uninhabited, and communities tend to settle along the coast on the southern islands.

Among the people you would meet in the Canadian Arctic are the Inuit—an aboriginal group who mainly live in northern areas of Canada. Many aspects of their lives were influenced by the freezing climate, although their way of life has changed greatly in the last century.

Traditionally, the Inuit lived in igloos made of snow and ice in the winter, and in tents made from animal skin in the summer. This was because there was no wood available to build houses. Some igloos could house up to 20 people!

Another aspect of life that is influenced by the climate is food. Because plants struggled to grow in the frozen ground of land inhabited by the Inuit, their diet consisted mainly of meat. They would fish and hunt for food. The staples of their diet were seals, walruses, whales, and fish.

Transportation was also a challenge. The Inuit people traveled using snowshoes, sleds pulled by dogs, and toboggans. The Inuit were also skilled at building boats. They used kayaks for hunting and bigger vessels to transport people and animals.

The Inuit language is called Inuktitut, although the name differs between the many dialects. Inuktitut is an official language along with English and French in Nunavut, which is the newest and largest settlement in Canada. The word *Inuit* means "the people," and *Inuk* is the term for one Inuit person. *Nunavut* means "our land."

HOW TO BUILD AN IGLOO

In *The Snow Bear*, Sara and her grandpa build an amazing igloo! Here's how to build your own when the snow falls.

1. Find an area with a lot of dry and hard-packed snow. The snow needs to be hard and without any layers; otherwise, it might crumble.

It's a good idea to build your igloo on a slope so you need fewer blocks.

2. Draw a circle in the snow and ask an adult to help cut blocks from the snow inside the circle using a snow saw or knife. The blocks need to be around 3 feet (1 m) long, 15 inches (38 cm) high, and 8 inches (20 cm) deep.

The smaller the circle, the warmer the igloo. Make sure the snow is at least 2 feet (0.6 m) deep so you have enough.

3. Place the blocks around your circle. As you work your way up, make sure the blocks decrease in size, overlap, and lean inward to create the dome.

Remember to cut ventilation holes in the roof and walls of the igloo to ensure that there is airflow.

You can use a stick to support the blocks until you're finished.

4. Once there's only an opening left at the top, place one final block to cover the gap. Save the biggest block for last to make sure you're covered.

5. Shovel loose snow onto the igloo and make sure you pack it into any gaps, inside and out.

6. You need to get in and out of your igloo! Some people make the entrance underground, but you can also make an entrance by cutting a hole into the wall.

And now you're ready to begin your own snowy adventure!

TURN THE PAGE FOR A
SNEAK PEEK AT

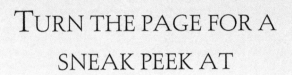

The
*Reindeer
Girl*

ANOTHER ICY
ADVENTURE IN THE
WINTER JOURNEYS SERIES!

CHAPTER ONE

Uncle Tomas glanced around at Lotta from the front seat of the car. "I know you really want to see your grandparents, and your great-grandmother. But the thing is, on the way from the airport to their house, we will go past the reindeer farm…."

Lotta gave a little gasp. "Right past it?" she asked, looking pleadingly between her mom and dad.

"Oh, I don't know…," Lotta's mom said, shaking her head doubtfully. "We're tired from the flight. And Mormor and Morfar and Oldemor will be at their house, waiting to see us."

Lotta nodded, trying not to look disappointed. This was her first trip to Norway, and although her grandparents— she called them by their Norwegian names, Mormor and Morfar—had been to the United States to visit them several times, she had never met her oldemor. Her great-grandmother was too frail to travel so far, but Lotta loved speaking to her on the phone. One of the reasons that they'd come to Tromsø this year was that Oldemor was going to be ninety, two days before Christmas. They were going to have a special party to celebrate.

But the reindeer.... For Lotta, they were one of the most exciting parts of the trip. They were all mixed up in her mind with the deep snow, and the cold, and the amazing Christmas spirit of everything. Even Tromsø airport had been full of beautiful Christmas decorations. And as soon as they had stepped outside, she had breathed in the crisp, freezing air and suddenly felt even more excited—which she hadn't thought was possible.

Ever since she could remember, her mom had told her stories about Oldemor and the reindeer. They were Lotta's favorite bedtime stories. After her mom had read her way through a stack of picture books, Lotta would always ask for one last story—"a real story now, about Erika and the reindeer."

Erika was her great-grandmother. When she was a little girl, she had lived in the forest with her family, who were Sami reindeer herders. Some of the time, she had slept in a tent that her family packed up in the mornings and carried on a sled. Erika had ridden on the sled when she was too tired to walk or ski, as her family traveled with the reindeer on their long journeys across the Finnmark highlands. It was a lot more interesting than living in a normal house and going to school every morning. In her mind, Lotta thought of Erika as the reindeer girl. She was desperate to meet her.

But she was desperate to meet the reindeer, too. There had been two life-size model ones in the airport, along with a lot of funny elves that Uncle Tomas had told her were called nisse. He said they were a special Norwegian thing, and Mormor had a bunch of little ones decorating the house. They had been sweet, but Lotta just wanted to see a real reindeer. She had read about them and tried to find out more about Oldemor's life as a reindeer herder. But it wasn't the same as meeting a real one.

"Actually, it was Oldemor's idea that we should stop at the farm," Uncle Tomas explained. "She said that when she spoke to Lotta on the telephone, she was so excited about the reindeer and asked so many questions. She  said that Lotta would understand all the stories she had to tell her much better if she met the reindeer first."

Lotta's mom laughed. "All right then. Between the two of them, I don't think we have much choice. I think Lotta might be more excited about seeing the reindeer than the family."

Lotta's cheeks turned pink. "That isn't true! I'm just excited about both."

"Good. We will stop at the reindeer farm then. None of our family herds reindeer in the same way that Oldemor did, Lotta," Uncle Tomas added. "Your great-uncle Aslak runs the farm, but he feeds the reindeer now. They don't roam wild."

Lotta nodded. "I guess nobody goes traveling with the reindeer now," she said, a little sadly.

"It's a hard life," Uncle Tomas said, shrugging. "But some families still do. They use snowmobiles mostly, though, not sleds. Ah, we're almost there. Just one more turn here." He guided the four-wheel drive off the main road, up a steep path and through a set of huge gates. There was a sign on them, but Lotta couldn't understand what it said. Her mom did talk to her in Norwegian and she knew a little bit, but she found it hard to read.

They climbed out of the car, and Lotta was thankful for her beautiful new red coat—it had been bought from a sporting goods store, and it was thick and padded, meant for skiing. Her mom had said that her old coat wouldn't be warm enough for the Norwegian winter. Even so, Lotta shivered a little as she pulled on her knitted mittens. Mormor had sent them to her when they had first decided to visit for Christmas. Mormor had said there was thick snow already and she would need them. Lotta loved the white snowflake pattern knitted into the red wool.

"Ah, you've come!" A huge bear of a man with a thick brown beard was hurrying out of the farmhouse toward them. "Little Lotta!" He hugged her, and he was so big that Lotta's feet lifted off the ground. "My mama says you are a reindeer girl, too, and I have to show you the reindeer."

His mama—that was Oldemor, Lotta realized. "Yes, please!" she told him, rather shyly. His English was amazingly good, although a little slow and thickly accented.

He took her hand, her mitten tiny inside his huge, fur-lined glove, and led them over to a shed that was built onto the side of the house. "I have two reindeer in here," he explained. "Both a little lame, so I brought them inside to recover." He opened the wooden door gently, and there was a scuffling noise from inside as two reindeer stood up in their stalls.

Lotta took a step back in surprise—somehow, she hadn't expected them to be quite so big. But then she smiled delightedly. "Oh, they're beautiful," she said. "Can I ... can I pet them?"

"Mm-hmm. These two are very tame. I have been feeding them while they are in here, so they are used to me. Here." Great-uncle Aslak tipped a handful of brown pellets into Lotta's mittened hand. "Give them these."

The reindeer snorted eagerly as they smelled the food and leaned over the metal fence, snuffling.

Lotta stretched out her hands a little cautiously, but the reindeer were both surprisingly gentle as they gobbled up the pellets. "They really like them!" she told her great-uncle.

HOLLY WEBB

Holly Webb started out as a children's book editor, and wrote her first series for the publisher she worked for. She has been writing ever since, with more than 100 books to her name. Holly lives in England with her husband, three young sons, and several cats who are always nosing around when she is trying to type on her laptop.

For more information
about Holly Webb visit:

www.holly-webb.com
www.tigertalesbooks.com